Honesty

Walt Disney's Pinocchio

Adapted by Guy Davis
Illustrated by the Disney Storybook Artists

Published by Louis Weber, C.E.O.
Publications International, Ltd.
7373 North Cicero Avenue, Lincolnwood, Illinois 60712

Ground Floor, 59 Gloucester Place, London W1U 8JJ
Customer Service: 1-800-595-8484 or customer_service@pilbooks.com

www.pilbooks.com

p i kids is a registered trademark of Publications International, Ltd.

ISBN-13: 978-1-4127-6243-4
ISBN-10: 1-4127-6243-X

Gepetto was a lonely wood carver who lived with his pets, Figaro and Cleo. Gepetto created amazing toys, music boxes, and clocks, but he was especially proud of his little wooden puppet.

"I will call *you* Pinocchio!" announced Gepetto.

Later that night, Gepetto looked up at a twinkling star. "More than anything else in the whole world, I wish that Pinocchio was a real boy," whispered Gepetto.

Just then, the Blue Fairy appeared. She was about to make Gepetto's wish come true!

“Prove yourself to be brave and truthful, and someday you’ll be a real boy!” announced the Blue Fairy. She waved her wand.

The puppet sprang to life!

“My son!” exclaimed Gepetto. “I am so proud!”

Gepetto picked up Pinocchio and danced around the workshop.

The Blue Fairy announced that Jiminy Cricket would be Pinocchio's conscience.

"What's a conscience?" asked Pinocchio.

"It's that little voice inside your head that tells you not to do things you shouldn't!" said Jiminy Cricket.

Unfortunately, Pinocchio didn't always listen to his conscience. The next day, Pinocchio promised he'd walk right to school. But along the way, he met Stromboli the puppeteer.

"Come with me, and I'll make you a star!" said the sneaky Stromboli.

"Don't do it!" cried Jiminy Cricket.

But Pinocchio didn't listen.

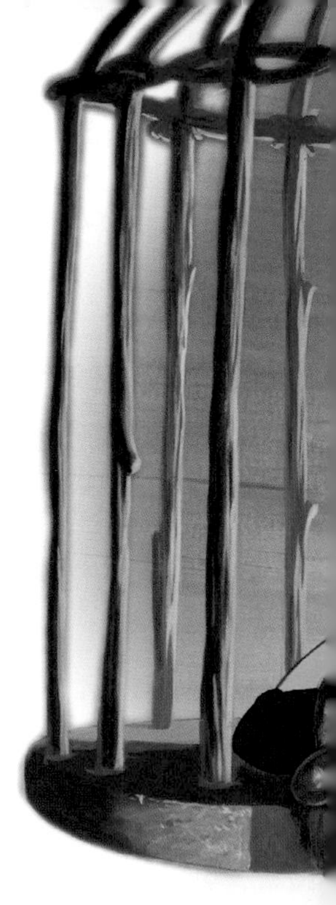

Instead, he jumped on stage and danced with the other puppets. Afterwards, Stromboli locked Pinocchio in a cage!

Fortunately, the Blue Fairy arrived to set Pinocchio free.

"Tell her," Jiminy Cricket said.

But instead of telling the truth, Pinocchio told a lie. Suddenly, Pinocchio's nose grew out like a huge branch!

"You haven't been telling the truth," said the Blue Fairy. "Remember, a lie will grow until it's as plain as the nose on your face!"

"I'll never tell a lie again," he cried. "Honest!"

But Pinocchio hadn't learned his lesson yet! The very next day, he skipped school and ran off to Pleasure Island.

"Pinocchio, this is a very bad place!" cried Jiminy Cricket.

Jiminy Cricket was right . . . because before his very eyes, all of the boys at Pleasure Island started turning into donkeys!

"What's happening to me?" asked Pinocchio, as he grew a tail. "I'm turning into a donkey, too! I should have told the truth!"

With Jiminy Cricket's help, Pinocchio escaped Pleasure Island. He ran quickly home, but Gepetto wasn't there. He had gone to search for Pinocchio and had been swallowed by Monstro the Whale!

Brave Pinocchio wasn't frightened. He ran to the ocean and jumped right in. Pinocchio was swallowed by the whale, too.

Pinocchio had a brilliant idea. They would build a fire and make Monstro sneeze. And that's just how Pinocchio rescued his father!

The Blue Fairy recognized that Pinocchio had finally learned to be brave and truthful. She waved her wand and turned Pinocchio into a real boy!

Safe and snug in his home, Pinocchio fell fast asleep next to Gepetto.

Looking up at the wishing star, Gepetto smiled. "Thank you for making my dream come true," Gepetto said sleepily.

"And thanks for teaching him to tell the truth!" added Jiminy Cricket.

Honesty

Honesty means telling the truth. Sometimes we're afraid to tell the truth because we don't want to get in trouble. But when Pinocchio didn't tell the truth, he only made things worse. Telling the truth isn't always easy, but it is always the right thing to do. Just ask Pinocchio!